Gracie Lou

Larissa Juliano

Illustrated by Stephen Adams

Dream Big!
♥ Lau Juliano

Archway Publishing books may be ordered through booksellers or by contacting:

Archway Publishing
1663 Liberty Drive
Bloomington, IN 47403
www.archwaypublishing.com
1 (888) 242-5904

Because of the dynamic nature of the Internet, any web addresses or links contained in
this book may have changed since publication and may no longer be valid. The views
expressed in this work are solely those of the author and do not necessarily reflect the
views of the publisher, and the publisher hereby disclaims any responsibility for them.

Any people depicted in stock imagery provided by Thinkstock are models,
and such images are being used for illustrative purposes only.
Certain stock imagery © Thinkstock.

ISBN: 978-1-4808-3322-7 (sc)
ISBN: 978-1-4808-3320-3 (hc)
ISBN: 978-1-4808-3321-0 (e)

Print information available on the last page.

Archway Publishing rev. date: 10/12/2016

To Chris...I want to
travel to all the pinholes
in the sky with you.

"You - you alone will have the stars as no one else has them...In one of the stars I shall be living. In one of them I shall be laughing. And so it will be as if all the stars were laughing, when you look at the sky at night...You - only you - will have stars that can laugh." - Antoine de Saint-Exupéry, The Little Prince

Gracie Lou was bored.

She was tired of her room.
All the toys were under her cousin's bed.
She couldn't possibly play dress up by
herself for one more minute.
And no one wanted to play. Ever.

Gracie Lou was bored....and sad.

That night, as she blinked her
sleepy eyes, Gracie Lou wished
she could escape her boredom
to a magical land far away...

When the sun set and the moon rose, her room lit up with a WHOOSH! A shooting star scooped up Gracie Lou and while they whizzed through all the sparkly stars, she could hardly believe her luck.

"And the walls became
the world all around."
Maurice Sendak,
Where the Wild Things Are

"Oh my, oh my! I *taste* something sweet!" she cried.

Sure enough, Gracie Lou's shooting star was approaching a CUPCAKE land! There were vanilla cupcakes, chocolate cupcakes, strawberry cupcakes, and even rainbow sprinkle cupcakes! She twirled around the sugary sweets, licked the frosting, and sampled the treats. Yum, yum, yum!

After awhile she declared, "Shooting star, shooting star, where are you? This has been fun, but I'm ready for something new!"

Her shooting star scooped her up and they raced through the sky. Soon, Gracie Lou began to feel flutters on her cheek! "Oh my, oh my! I *feel* something tickly!"

"I must endure the presence of a few caterpillars if
I wish to become acquainted with the butterflies"
Antoine de St. Exupery, The Little Prince

Gracie Lou leaped off her magical star and landed in a BUTTERFLY land! They had the most divine and vibrant colors. The breeze from their fluttery wings made Gracie Lou spin around and around. The butterflies lifted her higher than the tallest trees.

After awhile she exclaimed,
"Shooting star, shooting star, where
are you? This has been fun, but
I'm ready for something new!"

Her shooting star lifted her up and as she held on tight she wondered where they would go to next.

BRING, PING, ZING! "Oh my, oh my!
I *hear* something musical!" She was in
a MUSIC land! Gracie Lou jumped on
the enormous piano keys, played the shiny
trombone, and **jingle jangled** the biggest
tambourine she'd ever seen.

After awhile she called out, "Shooting star, shooting star, where are you? This has been fun, but I'm ready for something new!" Her shooting star zoomed over for Gracie Lou.

Once again, she was transported
through the dark sky. "Oh my, oh my!
I *see* something enormous!"

Dinosaurs of all different colors and
sizes were playing in the bushes below.
She was in a DINOSAUR land!
BANG, BOOM, BONG! A brontosaurus
nudged Gracie Lou. She slid down his
neck and giggled with glee! Playing 'Catch
the Rings' with a triceratops was her
favorite part of the night.

After awhile she shouted out, "Shooting star, shooting star, where are you? This has been fun, but I am ready for something new!"

Gracie Lou and her shooting star hurdled through the twinkly sky with more speed than ever before! "Oh my, oh my! I *smell* something LOVELY!"

She jumped off and ran into a FLOWER land! There were mountains of sunflowers, lilies, tulips, and roses. Their sweet scent tickled Gracie Lou's nose as she wove them in her hair. One purple rose stood out among the others. It had no thorns. Gracie Lou tucked it behind her ear. Soon she began to feel tired and her eyes very heavy...

"Shooting star, shooting star, where are you? This has been fun, but I think I am ready...to go home." Her shooting star dashed over.

As Gracie Lou snuggled into her bed she realized her imagination was the best boredom buster and adventure of all.

"Oh my, oh my...I wonder what tomorrow will bring."

"It's the time you spent on your rose that makes your rose so important...People have forgotten this truth, but you mustn't forget it. You become responsible forever for what you've tamed. You're responsible for your rose."
– Antoine de Saint-Exupéry, The Little Prince

About the Author

Larissa Juliano is an elementary and library teacher in upstate New York. She lives in her hometown with her husband and three young children. Besides teaching, her passion in life is writing books in hopes of inspiring children to use their imagination, especially through literature. This can be the very best travel ticket of all.

www.larissajuliano.com

To all the Gracie Lou's...
Dream Big.
You CAN do great things.

CPSIA information can be obtained
at www.ICGtesting.com
Printed in the USA
BVOW07*1133281016

465989BV00004B/4/P

9 781480 833203